If Pigs Could Fly

By Kenny LaFreniere • Illustrated by Fred Marvin

Based on the character Babe created by Dick King-Smith

Random House ⌂ New York

Copyright © 1999 by Universal Studios Publishing Rights, a division of Universal Studios Licensing, Inc. Babe, Babe: The Sheep Pig and related characters are copyrights and trademarks of Universal City Studios, Inc. All rights reserved under International and Pan-American Copyright Conventions. Published in the United States by Random House, Inc., New York, and simultaneously in Canada by Random House of Canada Limited, Toronto. Library of Congress Catalog Card Number: 98-66642 ISBN 0-679-89450-0 (trade) ; 0-679-99450-5 (lib. bdg.) www.randomhouse.com/kids
Printed in the United States of America 10 9 8 7 6 5 4 3 2 1
JELLYBEAN BOOKS is a trademark of Random House, Inc.

One windy morning on Hoggett's Farm,
Babe watched Ferdinand as he circled and
dipped above him.

Ferdinand came in for a landing.

"Oh, Ferdie," cried Babe. "I wish I could fly, too!"

"I like a pig with vision," said Ferdinand. "But you'll need some wings."

"Where did you get yours?" Babe asked.

"I was born with them," Ferdinand said.

So Babe went looking for wings.

"Excuse me, Ms. Hen," he said, "you have a fine set of wings. Could you tell me where you got them?"

But the only place the hen knew where wings could be found was inside an egg.

And what egg was big enough for Babe?

Babe wandered into the woods.

He stopped and
asked a sparrow…

a bluebird…

and a robin.

But none of them
knew where Babe
could get a set of wings
so he could fly.

Back at the barn, Babe asked the sheepdog if she could help. After all, her name *was* "Fly."

"Pigs aren't meant to fly, dear," Fly said. "That's just the way things are."

But Babe hated to give up.

"There must be a way," he said. "I just have to keep trying."

That afternoon, Farmer Hoggett wondered where his prized pig had gone.

He found Babe and Ferdinand out in the fields watching birds swoop and soar across the sky.

"I have an idea, Ferdie!" said Babe. "I'll flap my trotters as if they were wings! All I need is something high to jump off of!"

"I don't know about that," said
Ferdinand. "But you can always try."
    Babe looked around for something.
    "Aha!" he said. "The fence! I'll jump
from the fence."

Farmer Hoggett shook his head as he
watched his pig climb on top of the fence.
What in the world was Babe up to?

Babe jumped off the fence and flapped his
trotters with all his might!

But the only place Babe flew was...
straight down!

"Oof!" he said.

Now Farmer Hoggett thought he
knew what Babe was up to.
"Come, Pig," said Farmer Hoggett.
"I think I can help you."

Farmer Hoggett loaded Babe into
the truck and off they went.

"Hey, Ferdie! Look at me," shouted Babe. "I'm flying! I'm actually flying!"

"That's it, Babe. You're doing great!" called Ferdinand.

Farmer Hoggett looked at Babe. This was one pig that *could* fly.